Flying Over the Waves

a Night Stalkers 5E romance story
by
M. L. Buchman

Cover images:
Man and Woman Couple In Romantic Embrace
On Beach © Darren Baker
MH-6 Little Bird © San Andreas

Buchman Bookworks

Other works by M.L. Buchman

The Night Stalkers

MAIN FLIGHT
The Night Is Mine
I Own the Dawn
Wait Until Dark
Take Over at Midnight
Light Up the Night
Bring On the Dusk
By Break of Day

WHITE HOUSE HOLIDAY
Daniel's Christmas
Frank's Independence Day
Peter's Christmas
Zachary's Christmas
Roy's Independence Day
Damien's Christmas

AND THE NAVY
Christmas at Steel Beach
Christmas at Peleliu Cove

5E
Target of the Heart
Target Lock on Love
Target of Mine

Delta Force
Target Engaged
Heart Strike

<u>**Dead Chef Thrillers**</u>
Swap Out!
One Chef!
Two Chef!

<u>**SF/F Titles**</u>
Nara
Monk's Maze
The Me and Elsie Chronicles

Get a free Starter Library at:
www.mlbuchman.com

Don't Miss a Thing!

Sign up for M. L. Buchman's newsletter
today
and receive:
Release News
Free Short Stories
a Free Starter Library

Do it today. Do it now.
http://www.mlbuchman.com/newsletter/

1

"Since when do people get shot down on training missions?"

"At the moment I'm more worried about the North Sea," her copilot shot back.

Night Stalkers Chief Warrant 3 Debbie Rosenthal decided that he had a point.

Tonight the North Sea was being thrashed by a mid-December Force 9 severe gale—that felt like a Force 12 hurricane the way it shook her helicopter. It slammed them around in all three dimensions with the ease of a beach ball. Command had decided that gale force winds in the fifty mile-an-hour range was a good excuse for training.

Debbie hadn't argued.

First off, Command wouldn't care what a mere CW3 said any more than her father had. He'd disowned her the day she'd joined the Army rather than marrying a good Jewish boy.

Second, such an on-the-edge flight fit her own idea of a good skills freshener, well, other than being slammed about the sky. The Night Stalkers of the US Army's 160th SOAR 5th Battalion E Company were tasked with flying their helicopters through every form of ugly and it was great practice—when they weren't shooting at you.

When they weren't *supposed* to be shooting at you.

From a thousand feet up, flying over the North Sea in the middle of the night had merely been a good ride. From a thousand feet up over freezing waves two-to-three stories tall, breaking in huge sheets of slashing spray—with no engine—it was far less amusing.

The external cameras were good enough to paint the picture across the inside of her visor in horrifying detail despite the darkness.

"Are you sure we were shot?" It was a dumb question, but it came out anyway.

Chief Warrant 2 Silvan Exeter just pointed at the hole in their windshield that was currently shooting a stream of cold rainwater between them. The radio and engine had vanished at the same moment as their engine. The miracle was that neither of them had been hurt.

The other Little Bird in their flight hadn't been so lucky, but she couldn't think about Junker and Tank at the moment.

Their two-helicopter flight had passed above a fishing trawler seventy miles off Aberdeen, Scotland. At the time (all of sixty seconds ago) it had seemed like a good idea to do hover practice over a clear reference point. Could they hold position, in formation, directly above the trawler no matter what the wind and waves were doing? The trawler probably wouldn't even know they were there, testing hover skills in the night.

Thirty seconds ago, the trawler had unveiled a Soviet ZU-23mm anti-aircraft gun.

Not fishing trawler. Russian *spy* trawler.

Her aircraft was damaged first. Then the ship had swung fire against the other Little Bird and held it there. The second aircraft had plummeted out of the sky, no attempt at control or recovery. They were swinging back to finish her off as well, but it took too long. By then Silvan had fired a trio of Hydra 70 rockets into the trawler.

Debbie felt the billow of the massive explosion despite the gale-level wind. Everything above sea level was erased—gun, gunner, the entire trawler. In her infrared night vision—which was still working by some miracle—she could see the remains of the hull were awash and would sink soon. Even if it was an act of idiocy, it was also an act of war. There was going to be hell to pay if anyone lived to report it.

There were only two of them left out here in the middle of the North Sea and the odds didn't look good.

Per protocol, Silvan kept calling out the engine restart procedures while going through the emergency checklist…not that anything was likely to work.

Any further disbelief that her subconscious was tossing out upon the waters would have to wait until later. After she didn't die.

Debbie could feel the heavy weight of the wind shuddering through the controls.

No hydraulic assist in a MH-6M Little Bird.

No crew chiefs in back performing some miracle, like fabricating a new engine out of old bullet casings in the sixty seconds she'd be able to keep them aloft. That was the land of Black Hawks and Chinooks. In the Little Bird, it was just the two of them.

Autorotation was dicey at the best of times. Autorotation with winds gusting past fifty and nowhere to land just wasn't going to work.

"Can you reach the raft?"

Silvan hesitated in mid-"Ignition-test on, negative indicators, Ignition-start press and hold, negative start." She'd already lost half her altitude and was descending through five hundred feet. They were at max glide time, minus a factor of extra speed so that the storm didn't flip them too easily. Better faster with less flight time than upside down with only seconds to go. Head-on into the wind to get maximum lift…it didn't matter where they went, so she wasn't worried about distance.

No one ever survived bailing out of a crashing

helicopter, so the requirement to carry the small raft on long crossings was silly, but it was on the books. Ditching was something you only survived if balanced perfectly with no rotors catching the water—and in dead calm weather. And then only if you were lucky. Actually, there were survivors during storm ditchings, but they were very rare—more statistical anomaly than fact. A Little Bird wasn't some old-style US Coast Guard HH-3F Pelican designed to float. They were going to sink so fast that hitting the water was barely going to slow them down.

"I can only reach the raft if I go outside," he sounded grim. A Little Bird had a cockpit small enough that Debbie had never understood how two men could fly one. At least her shoulders were narrow enough that they only bumped together half the time they were aloft. The back two seats were even smaller. "Outside" meant stepping out onto the skid, shuffling backward in a roaring wind, and yanking the rear door open—all while she was busy pitching and yawing like a drunkard on a bender.

"Three hundred feet," was the only answer she had for Silvan.

2

"Silvan? Like Tolkien's elves? You're tall enough to be one." Debbie leaned back against the nose of her Little Bird, warm in the April afternoon. She looked up at the new guy—six-one, maybe six-two, a long way up. The sun caught his blond hair and made it shine. He was also slender like an elf, except for a very nice set of soldier's shoulders.

"Mom was a fan. And with our last name being Exeter... Exeter College was Tolkien's alma mater. I never stood a chance," new guy shrugged. *Very* nice shoulders. Good smile too. Debbie liked good smiles.

"I didn't know there were elves in the Army. Something's wrong with your ears though."

He fell for it and actually reached up to touch

7

them, before he sighed. "Not pointed. Right. Maybe I'm a deformed elf."

"Or a reformed one." Not one bit deformed from where she was watching. Hide his ears and he'd make a very fair Legolas in the Lord of the Rings movies. His hair was still Army-short, but maybe she could corrupt him. Her own was down to her shoulders. Very un-Army, but very Night Stalkers.

The Night Stalkers' customers—Delta Force especially—let their hair go long to help them blend in when infiltrating undercover. And there wasn't a Delta operator who didn't also glory in the chance to say "up yours" to the military hierarchy that they'd voluntarily sworn to serve to the death. A lot of the fliers in the 160th SOAR took their close association with Delta and SEAL Team 6 as an excuse to let their own hair get long.

"Let it grow out. That'll hide the defect." Because otherwise he was damn near perfect. Not gorgeous, though not homely by a long stretch, but rather cute, strong, and funny. "Besides, you'd look good in long hair."

He squatted down, flexing arms and clenching fists, and grimaced horribly.

"What's wrong?"

He looked like he was holding himself back from pummeling something.

Or maybe trying to give birth right there on the runway in front of her helicopter.

"Is it working?" His voice little more than a grunt.

"Is what working?"

He stopped whatever it was he was doing and patted the top of his head. "Crap!"

"What?"

"A beautiful woman tells me to grow my hair long, I wondered if I could hurry up the process. You know, like the Incredible Hulk." When he resumed the hunched, grimace-riddled stance— she recognized it, right out of the movies.

"An angry roar and you've got it nailed."

And he roared! Right there in the middle of Fort Rucker, Alabama airfield. Other crews were turning startled looks in their direction, but Silvan didn't seem to care.

When he finished, he stood up normally, as if nothing had happened and half the field wasn't watching him, and patted the top of his head again.

Then he whispered a soft, "Damn! No change."

Debbie would have burst out laughing at that moment if she could have, he was awfully cute.

But she couldn't.

Because she knew that in that instant, whether or not she was his commander, she was gone on him.

3

Silvan popped loose his harness then turned to her.

"Remember, jump into the top of a wave. If you jump into a trough from a height, you're going to fall that extra thirty feet."

They were crossing down through the two-hundred-foot mark and the difference from crest to trough was looking more like five stories than three. These waves were huge.

"After I get the raft, we jump together, from opposite sides," he shouted for emphasis.

"Roger that. Go!"

And he *was* gone: yanking free the data-and-communications umbilical cord to his helmet, jamming open the door with a shoulder, then leveraging his way out onto the bucking skid. The wind roared and swirled about her for a moment before the wind slammed it closed.

She should have said something.

Something to show that she cared.

That he was important.

That even though they'd never had a chance, she wished they had.

A vicious gust slapped them hard. She managed to lean her side of the Little Bird into it. It cost her some altitude, but it would spare Silvan the worst of it.

She was way too busy to look to see if he was still there, clinging to the outside of the helo.

One-fifty.

The wind's roar in the cabin returned with double the volume.

The rear door was open. Silvan was still with her.

"I've got the raft!" Debbie could barely hear his shout.

"Keep growing your hair!" *Stupid! Stupid! Stupid!*

That was going to be the last thing she ever said to him?

4

"Keep trying," Debbie managed past a constricted throat, trying not to make their first meeting too awkward. "Six months tops and it should cover those awkward ears."

"Mom would like you."

"She doesn't like the kind of trollops you normally drag home?" Maybe it was the Alabama heat shimmering off the airfield that melted what little manners she normally maintained.

Silvan had the decency to laugh despite her catty remark. "Not much. Would you believe that some of them haven't even read *The Hobbit?*"

"Horrors!"

"Indeed," he agreed.

And that had set the tone for their entire first meeting. They'd shared stories of trainings and missions, of joining the military and that they were each nearing their first decade of service.

She'd felt bad about not sharing her past, but Silvan made it easy with stories of his own. His family life wasn't some picture postcard, but it wasn't a dysfunctional TV sitcom either. Engineer mom, professor dad, older sister lawyer with one kid and a divorce.

For eight months they'd flown together, laughed together, and survived every mission thrown at them.

In eight months he'd never done a single thing to reverse her initial impression.

Silvan was a seriously decent guy who easily kept up with her quirky sense of humor. Even better, together they forced each other to become better fliers.

It seemed they'd done everything together— except one.

5

Well, two things. They'd also never died together but, odds on, they were about to.

She didn't dare take a hand off either of the controls, so she couldn't do anything to prepare for the jump except rehearse the steps in her head: release controls, punch harness release with one hand, then yank out the helmet's umbilical cord while opening the door with the other. Thankfully, she and Silvan were already wearing inflatable life vests on top of their standard gear.

With her left thumb she flicked the landing light switch on the end of the collective control. The sudden glare revealed a nightmare landscape of sheeting spray and breaking waves covered with foaming spindrift.

A wave crested fifty feet below her.

No time to grab anything, just enough to—

Down in the trough was what remained of the spy trawler's hull.

A flat structure. The lowest deck had survived the blast. Now just barely awash.

If she could land there, even for a moment, their chances of survival were going to skyrocket.

6

"Why don't you have a past?"

Debbie sat slouched beside Silvan after a brutally long mission deep into Libya to take part in wiping out an al-Qaeda camp. They'd made it back to the USS *Harry S. Truman* aircraft carrier with the first of the predawn light. By unspoken mutual consent, they'd found a corner of the hangar deck with a view out over the ship's wake. There they'd collapsed and settled in to watch the sunrise over the Mediterranean.

For a long time—from dark blue to soft pink—Debbie just let the waves hold her attention. She felt their beat in her aching body. Little Birds were meant for two-hour out-and-back operations. Muhammad Ali's "Sting like a bee"—that was a Little Bird's sweet spot. Which fit her perfectly, as her full name, Deborah, meant "bee" in Hebrew. Long missions took their toll. Ones long enough to require multiple refueling stops really took the honey right out of her mood.

Silvan waited her out. He was good at that, sensing her mood and letting her have that space. There was so much to appreciate about him aside from his skills as a flier.

"You weren't born the day you joined the Army." He was also good at calling her on her own bullshit avoidance, even if she didn't appreciate it.

"I'm a bad Jewish daughter. I didn't marry a Jew. I didn't even go into business or law. Except my family isn't just Jewish, they're Orthodox Haredi. It means we aren't supposed to even mingle with non-Jewish cultures."

"So the Army ticked them off. Is that why you joined?"

Debbie had to smile, "Can't say that I minded that aspect of it, but no. There was a boy at our *yeshiva*—think Jewish high school that only reluctantly allows girls—Moshe. He was by far the best of us all. But he was in the wrong place at the wrong time—a mugging that escalated badly. Anyway, he was dead before they got him to the hospital. That was the moment I truly became aware of the outside world. The more I learned…" she couldn't finish the sentence.

"The more you felt a need to fix it?"

She could only nod. She didn't even mind Silvan's habit of being able to finish her sentences because he was always right when he did. The waves of her life kept flowing by like the sunlit wake of the aircraft carrier as she watched—no way to ever hold onto them. No way to ever bring them back.

7

"*Hull!*" *Debbie shouted as* loudly as she could.

By the wind's roar—now augmented by the breaking waves—she knew the rear door was still open and Silvan was still with her.

If he responded, she couldn't hear it. But the roar filled her ears—they'd jump together.

She flew so close above the next crest that she could have stepped out onto the wavetop. A second later, she was over the yawning chasm of a trough. But the hull had survived or at least a piece of it.

Forty.

Thirty.

At twenty she reefed back on the cyclic hard, a final flare to dump speed and trade it in for a momentary, unsustainable hover.

A last kick of the rudder pedals.

Impact!

More of a crash than a landing onto the trawler, but it had worked.

Now all her years of training kicked in.

Not turning to Silvan—not even hesitating to be surprised that she was still alive—she slapped, pulled, opened, and leapt out.

She dove into the freezing sea and slammed against the two feet of the trawler's outer wooden hull, then collapsed onto the flat deck. She ate a mouthful of saltwater as she groaned at the abuse. A glance up revealed the Little Bird's rotors still windmilling at lethal speed.

The next wave began to lift the hull and the helo fell, tipping toward her. Nowhere to dive. Her life vest—which had auto-inflated on contact with the water—kept her pinned to the surface like a bug about to be squashed.

Through the driving sleet and icy spray, she saw the blades slash into the water less than an arm's length past her position. Without the engine driving them, they stopped almost immediately.

She felt like a lion in a carbon-fiber blade cage: the body of her helo behind her and the blades driven down into the sea in front.

Then the wave's face went near enough to vertical for the helicopter to roll off the hull. She actually banged her helmet on some part of the helo as it tumbled by—driving her face once more into the frigid wash of water now two feet deep over the sinking deck. Her helo disappeared beneath the waves.

Just because the boat's hull was wallowing so deeply, didn't abate the wave's vehemence. In a cloud of slashing spray and biting wind, it flipped the hull over this time. Catapulting her aside with the ease of a rag doll, she landed clear of its tumbling mass.

Too much for the remains of the trawler, it finally plunged for the depths. Caught in its vortex rush of sinking water, she was dragged deep beneath the surface.

She swam hard, letting the life vest tell her which way was up and broke the surface just before her lungs burst from holding her breath so hard. She slid down the back of the wave.

A light blinked in the darkness.

Silvan.

Just going over the crest of the next wave over.

He might as well be a mile away.

8

Silvan wiped the water out of his eyes for the hundredth time since he'd plunged into the icy North Sea. Alone, he rode over the wave and down the far side, bobbing as lightly as a cork.

If ever there was a pilot to fly with, it was Chief Warrant Deborah Rosenthal.

Which was exactly how he felt every time he got close to her. He'd like to have gotten much closer, but the Army wasn't the only one against that. Their rank wasn't an issue, but the fact that she was his superior officer was. He hadn't wanted to risk not flying with her in the future.

There was also something within her. Something…torn. It had kept him pushed to a distance and he'd done his best to respect that.

And now he didn't know if he'd ever have a

chance to see past whatever that was, or even to thank her for saving him.

Had she died in that final act?

There was no way he should be alive, but she'd been masterful. Landing for those crucial few seconds on the hull had absolutely saved his life.

He'd felt the skid hit the boat's hull through the heels of his boots. The next instant he had kicked backward as hard as he could, flinging himself clear. With the two-foot-long life raft bag clutched hard to his chest, he hadn't sunk more than a few feet.

Then he'd watched in horror as first the helicopter and then the entire boat hull flipped over on where she would have jumped clear. If she even survived the landing.

He wiped his face again and tried to kick himself in a circle, hoping against hope that he'd spot the light from her life vest.

Night.

Screaming wind.

Pitch-black, overcast night.

Yet, he could see shades of the gale's madness— the waves as they ripped past him.

No thought to grab the night-vision goggles that he kept stowed under the console. When attached to the helicopter, everything he needed was projected on the inside of his visor.

Next time, if there was a next time, he would remember to grab his goddamn NVGs.

A glimmer?

He watched closely over the next wave crest.

Definitely a brightness beyond the next wave. The only light in the night, he'd take hope from that.

He hooked the uninflated life raft to his belt on a short tether so that it would trail behind him and began swimming.

9

Debbie had lost sight of Silvan. No matter how hard she swam, he seemed to slip farther and farther away.

She made sure that her emergency radio beacon was blinking, indicating it was crying for help, but how long was rescue going to take to reach her? She was fifty miles from land in every direction in the midst of a brutal winter storm. The first shot had killed the helo's radios and there'd been no time to try the handhelds.

Now, to hear her little beacon, it would take a very lucky satellite or someone flying directly over her and listening for her signal. How long before Search and Rescue came looking? Too long.

It was just her and Silvan.

No, it was just her.

That thought slammed in with a punch harder than the icy ocean seeping into her foul-weather flight gear. Next time she flew, she'd wear a goddamn dry suit.

No Silvan. She hadn't let him get too close to her because…

A wave crest slapped and tumbled her. Rather than burying her under, the wind ripping at the water was enough to blow her through the air for a short distance and bury her face-first into the water, again. She resurfaced.

Because she was an idiot.

Silvan Exeter was the best man she was never going to meet again. Impossibly, even better than Moshe who had been swept backward by the tide of time as well.

She'd lost all sense of direction when the wave had tossed her.

She treaded water, slowly turning in a circle, searching for any sign of hope. Deborah the Prophetess had led the biblical legions against the oppression of King Jabin and his military general Sisera. The latter had fallen to a woman pounding a tent peg through his temple while he rested. Well, Debbie didn't have a tent peg, a mallet, or the knowledge of a prophetess of the Lord God.

All she had was—

A shining beacon in the distance. A tiny flashing light.

Attached to a man plunging down a wave face easily five stories tall.

As he swam *in her direction.*

A rescue swimmer? Already?

No!

Leaving the chill that had threatened to encase her behind a solid wall, she dug into the waves, speeding toward Silvan.

10

Both cold, gasping for breath from the hard swim necessary to fight their way together, and lost in the North Sea—the first thing they had done was kiss.

It had been sloppy, hurried, freezing, and in moments they were battered apart except for the death grip on the front ring of each others' vests.

But it changed Silvan's world.

It hadn't been a kiss of "so glad to see you."

Their coming together had been an "Oh my god, I thought you were dead!"

It took a coordinated effort, but they deployed the raft and managed to climb in before it blew away. It was small comfort in the heavy storm—it didn't stay dry, but at least it remained upright. Between judicious bailing and unfurling the canopy, they finally were reasonably secure.

The only way they could keep from being slammed together was by holding tightly to each other. It was something that Silvan had wanted to do for so long that it was hard to believe it was finally happening. Not how he'd imagined it, but holding her tight might just be the best thing to ever happen to him.

"You aren't going to die!" Debbie shook him by her hold on his vest.

It seemed an odd statement as this was perhaps the safest they'd been in over an hour.

"You aren't!" She shook him again.

"You're awfully strong for someone who isn't an elf."

She shook him again, though not as hard. As if she could anchor her words in his chest.

If they hadn't been deep in the comparative calm inside the high-sided raft, he wouldn't have heard her next statement.

"I'm not wrong this time. I can't be. You're going to live." Then she buried her face against his shoulder and simply hung on.

There, with the waves raging by dozens of feet above them, he knew he had found the missing piece, the tear in her world.

Moshe. He wasn't "some boy" who had died and changed the course of Debbie Rosenthal's life.

She'd been there. Held him while he died,

telling him he was going to live. Her boyfriend? Her lover?

"Did he save you?"

Her nod told him the rest of the story. Moshe had died to protect her and she was repaying him by protecting everyone else that she could.

Silvan held her tightly, and she let him.

An eternity of howling winds and bailing out icy seawater later, a big C-130 Hercules turboprop roared by close overhead, soaring through the first light of day. It had sniffed out the track of their emergency locators.

The satellite phone had been useless, the wave troughs too deep to allow even the time to place a call. Their handheld radios were only good for line-of-sight communications. But now with the big plane circling above, he pulled out the radio and told them they were safe and uninjured…and that there was no point searching for the other two pilots. The rest of the report would be for the company commander's ears alone. He could decide who to contact about the spy trawler.

Within the hour, a helo and a rescue swimmer would arrive to hoist them off the waves. The plane promised to stay on station despite the turbulence their crew must be suffering.

11

Debbie lay quiet now, comfortable inside the circle of Silvan's arms while they awaited the rescue team that would pluck them from the sea. Their helmets kept the worst of the howling wind at bay.

"You don't need to worry about protecting me."

Silvan's shouted words were like a benediction. He might not understand that she hadn't had a single thought of her own survival during the crash landing—she'd been shocked when she'd survived. But she'd known without a doubt that getting down on that hull had improved Silvan's chances of survival. That was all that had mattered.

But maybe he was right. She didn't need to protect him as if he could be erased from existence at any moment. He'd survived the gunfire and crash just as they'd survived dozens of missions.

When it was their time, like Junker and Tank, it would be their time.

Until then—

Debbie sat up as much as the pitching raft would allow and studied Silvan's face. A few strands of his beautiful blond hair were finally long enough peek out from under the edge of his helmet.

"I've got an idea."

His frown said that he couldn't hear her.

She braced herself against his shoulders by curling her fists around his vest's armholes. Then she leaned in and repeated her shout between his right cheek and the edge of his helmet.

"Bring it on, lady. If it's a good one, I'll put in a good word for you with the elf king." His breath was warm against her chilled cheek.

"How about we just worry about protecting each other?"

"Sounds like a good plan." Then Silvan's face sobered, "How long were you thinking?" He had to repeat that more loudly.

When he did, Debbie couldn't help but feel the warmth in her heart despite the hail and spray currently battering at them. "How long have you got?"

Silvan's easy smile started slow but built big and then disappeared from view when he kissed her to seal the bargain.

Debbie let her heart ride the wave as it lifted the two of them out of the trough and over the top together.

She hoped they had a long, long time.

About the Author

M.L. Buchman started the first of, what is now over 50 novels and as many short stories, while flying from South Korea to ride his bicycle across the Australian Outback. Part of a solo around the world trip that ultimately launched his writing career.

All three of his military romantic suspense series—The Night Stalkers, Firehawks, and Delta Force—have had a title named "Top 10 Romance of the Year" by the American Library Association's Booklist. NPR and Barnes & Noble have named other titles "Top 5 Romance of the Year." In 2016 he was a finalist for Romance Writers of America prestigious RITA award. He also writes: contemporary romance, thrillers, and fantasy.

Past lives include: years as a project manager, rebuilding and single-handing a fifty-foot sailboat, both flying and jumping out of airplanes, and he has designed and built two houses. He is now making his living as a full-time writer on the Oregon Coast with his beloved wife and is constantly amazed at what you can do with a degree in Geophysics. You may keep up with his writing and receive a free starter e-library by subscribing to his newsletter at:

www.mlbuchman.com

If you enjoyed this story, you might also enjoy:

Target of the Heart (excerpt)
-a Night Stalkers 5E novel-

Major Pete Napier hovered his MH-47G Chinook helicopter ten kilometers outside of Lhasa, Tibet and a mere two inches off the tundra. A mixed action team of Delta Force and The Activity—the slipperiest intel group on the planet—flung themselves aboard.

The additional load sent an infinitesimal shift in the cyclic control in his right hand. The hydraulics to close the rear loading ramp hummed through the entire frame of the massive helicopter. By the time his crew chief could reach forward to slap an "all secure" signal against his shoulder, they were already ten feet up and fifty out. That was enough altitude. He kept the nose down as he clawed for speed in the thin air at eleven thousand feet.

"Totally worth it," one of the D-boys announced as soon as he was on the Chinook's internal intercom.

He'd have to remember to tell that to the two Black Hawks flying guard for him...when they were in a friendly country and could risk a radio transmission. This deep inside China—or rather Chinese-held territory as the CIA's mission-briefing spook had insisted on calling it—radios attracted attention and were only used to avoid imminent death and destruction.

"Great, now I just need to get us out of this alive."

"Do that, Pete. We'd appreciate it."

He wished to hell he had a stealth bird like the one that had gone into bin Laden's compound. But the one that had crashed during that raid had been blown up. Where there was one, there were always two, but the second had gone back into hiding as thoroughly as if it had never existed. He hadn't heard a word about it since.

The Tibetan terrain was amazing, even if all

he could see of it was the monochromatic green of night vision. And blackness. The largest city in Tibet lay a mere ten kilometers away and they were flying over barren wilderness. He could crash out here and no one would know for decades unless some yak herder stumbled upon them. Or were yaks in Mongolia? He was a corn-fed, white boy from Colorado, what did he know about Tibet? Most of the countries he'd flown into on black ops missions he'd only seen at night anyway.

While moving very, very fast.

Like now.

The inside of his visor was painted with overlapping readouts. A pre-defined terrain map, the best that modern satellite imaging could build made the first layer. This wasn't some crappy, on-line, look-at-a-picture-of-your-house display. Someone had a pile of dung outside their goat pen? He could see it, tell you how high it was, and probably say if they were pygmy goats or full-size LaManchas by the size of their shit-pellets if he zoomed in.

On top of that were projected the forward-looking infrared camera images. The FLIR imaging gave him a real-time overlay, in case someone had put an addition onto their goat shed since the last satellite pass, or parked their tractor across his intended flight path.

His nervous system was paying autonomic attention to that combined landscape. He also compensated for the thin air at altitude as he instinctively chose when to start his climb over said goat shed or his swerve around it.

It was the third layer, the tactical display that had most of his attention. At least he and the two Black Hawks flying escort on him were finally on the move.

To insert this deep into Tibet, without passing over Bhutan or Nepal, they'd had to add wingtanks on the Black Hawks' hardpoints where he'd much rather have a couple banks of Hellfire missiles. Still, they had 20mm chain guns and the crew chiefs had miniguns which was some comfort.

While the action team was busy infiltrating the capital city and gathering intelligence on the particularly brutal Chinese assistant administrator, he and his crews had been squatting out in the wilderness under a camouflage net designed to make his helo look like just another god-forsaken Himalayan lump of granite.

Command had determined that it was better for the helos to wait on site through the day than risk flying out and back in. He and his crew had stood shifts on guard duty, but none of them had slept. They'd been flying together too long to have any new jokes, so they'd played a lot of cribbage. He'd long ago ruled no gambling on a mission, after a fistfight had broken out about a bluff hand that cost a Marine three hundred and forty-seven dollars. Marines hated losing to Army no matter how many times it happened. They'd had to sit on him for a long time before he calmed down.

Tonight's mission was part of an on-going campaign to discredit the Chinese "presence" in Tibet on the international stage—as if occupying the country the last sixty years didn't count toward ruling, whether invited or not. As usual, there was a crucial vote coming up at the U.N.—that, as usual, the Chinese could be guaranteed to ignore. However, the ever-hopeful CIA was in a hurry to make sure that any damaging information that they could validate was disseminated as thoroughly as possible prior to the vote.

Not his concern.

His concern was, were they going to pass over some Chinese sentry post at their top speed of a hundred and ninety-six miles an hour? The sentries would then call down a couple Shenyang J-16 jet fighters that could hustle along at Mach 2 to fry his sorry ass. He knew there was a pair of them parked at Lhasa along with some older gear that would be just as effective against his three helos.

"Don't suppose you could get a move on, Pete?"

"Eat shit, Nicolai!" He was a good man to have as a copilot. Pete knew he was holding on too tight, and Nicolai knew that a joke was the right way to ease the moment.

He, Nicolai, and the four pilots in the two Black Hawks had a long way to go tonight and he'd never make it if he stayed so tight on the controls that he could barely maneuver. Pete eased off and felt his fingers tingle with the rush of returning blood. They dove down into gorges and followed them as long as they dared. They hugged cliff walls at every opportunity to decrease their radar profile. And they climbed.

That was the true danger—they would be up near the helos' limits when they crossed over the backbone of the Himalayas in their rush for India. The air was so rarefied that they burned fuel at a prodigious rate. Their reserve didn't allow for any extended battles while crossing the border…not for any battle at all really.

# # #

It was pitch dark outside her helicopter when Captain Danielle Delacroix stamped on the left rudder pedal while giving the big Chinook right-directed control on the cyclic. It tipped her most of the way onto her side, but let her continue in a straight line. A Chinook's rotors were sixty feet across—front to back they overlapped to make the spread a hundred feet long. By cross-controlling her bird to tip it, she managed to execute a straight line between two mock pylons only thirty feet apart. They were made of thin cloth so they wouldn't down the helo if you sliced one—she was the only trainee to not have cut one yet.

At her current angle of attack, she took up less than a half-rotor of width, just twenty-four feet. That left her nearly three feet to either side, sufficient as she was moving at under a hundred knots.

The training instructor sitting beside her in the copilot's seat didn't react as she swooped through the training course at Fort Campbell, Kentucky. Only child of a single mother, she was used to providing her own feedback loops, so she didn't expect anything else. Those who expected outside validation rarely survived the SOAR induction testing, never mind the two years of training that followed.

As a loner kid, Danielle had learned that self-motivated congratulations and fun were much easier to come by than external ones. She'd spent innumerable hours deep in her mind as a pre-teen superheroine. At twenty-nine she was well on her way to becoming a real life one, though Helo-girl had never been a character she'd thought of in her youth.

External validation or not, after two years of training with the U.S. Army's 160th Special Operations Aviation Regiment she was ready for some action. At least *she* was convinced that she was. But the trainers of Fort Campbell, Kentucky had not signed off on anyone in her trainee class yet. Nor had they given any hint of when they might.

She ducked ten tons of racing Chinook

under a bridge and bounced into a near vertical climb to clear the power line on the far side. Like a ride on the toboggan at Terrassee Dufferin during Le Carnaval de Québec, only with five thousand horsepower at her fingertips. Using her Army signing bonus—the first money in her life that was truly hers—to attend *Le Carnaval* had been her one trip back to her birthplace since her mother took them to America when she was ten.

To even apply to SOAR required five years of prior military rotorcraft experience. She had applied after seven years because of a chance encounter—or rather what she'd thought was a chance encounter at the time.

Captain Justin Roberts had been a top Chinook pilot, the one who had convinced her to switch from her beloved Black Hawk and try out the massive twin-rotor craft. One flight and she'd been a goner, begging her commander until he gave in and let her cross over to the new platform. Justin had made the jump from the 10th Mountain Division to the 160th SOAR not long after that.

Then one night she'd been having pizza in Watertown, New York a couple miles off the 10th's base at Fort Drum.

"Danielle?" Justin had greeted her with the surprise of finding a good friend in an unexpected place. Danielle had liked Justin—even if he was a too-tall, too-handsome cowboy and completely knew it. But "good friend" was unusual for Danielle, with anyone, and Justin came close.

"Captain Roberts," as a dry greeting over the top edge of her Suzanne Brockmann novel didn't faze him in the slightest.

"Mind if I join ya?" A question he then answered for himself by sliding into the opposite seat and taking a slice of her pizza. She been thinking of taking the leftovers back to base, but that was now an idle thought.

"Are you enjoying life in SOAR?" she did her best to appear a normal, social human, a skill she'd learned by rote. *Greeting someone you knew after a time apart? Ask a question about them.* "They treating you well?"

"Whoo-ee, you have no idea, Danielle," his voice was smooth as…well, always…so she wouldn't think about it also sounding like a pickup line. He was beautiful, but didn't interest her; the outgoing ones never did.

"Tell me." *Men love to talk about themselves, so let them.*

And he did. But she'd soon forgotten about her novel, and would have forgotten the pizza if he hadn't reminded her to eat.

His stories shifted from intriguing to fascinating. There was a world out there that she'd been only peripherally aware of. The Night Stalkers of the 160th SOAR weren't simply better helicopter pilots, they were the most highly-trained and best-equipped ones on the planet. Their missions were pure razor's edge and black-op dark.

He'd left her with a hundred questions and enough interest to fill out an application to the 160th. Being a decent guy, Justin even paid for the pizza after eating half.

The speed at which she was rushed into testing told her that her meeting with Justin hadn't been by chance and that she owed him more than half a pizza next time they met. She'd asked after him a couple of times since she'd made it past the qualification exams—and the examiners' brutal interviews that had left her questioning her sanity, never mind her ability.

"Justin Roberts is presently deployed, ma'am," was the only response she'd gotten.

Now that she was through training—almost, had to be soon, didn't it?—Danielle realized that was probably less of an evasion and more likely to do with the brutal op tempo the Night Stalkers maintained. The SOAR 1st Battalion had just won the coveted Lt. General Ellis D. Parker awards for Outstanding Combat Aviation Battalion *and* Aviation Battalion of the Year. They'd been on deployment every single day of the last year, actually of the last decade-plus since 9/11.

The very first Special Forces boots on the ground in Afghanistan were delivered that October by the Night Stalkers and nothing had slacked off since. Justin might be in the 5th battalion D company, but they were just as heavily assigned as the 1st.

Part of their training had included tours in Afghanistan. But unlike their prior deployments, these were brief, intense, and then they'd be back in the States pushing to integrate their new skills.

SOAR needed her training to end and so did she.

Danielle was ready for the job, in her own, inestimable opinion. But she wasn't going to get there until the trainers signed off that she'd reached fully mission-qualified proficiency.

The Fort Campbell training course was never set up the same from one flight to the next, but it always had a time limit. The time would be short and they didn't tell you what it was. So she drove the Chinook for all it was worth like Regina Jaquess waterskiing her way to U.S. Ski Team Female Athlete of the Year.

The Night Stalkers were a damned secretive lot, and after two years of training, she understood why. With seven years flying for the 10th, she'd thought she was good.

She'd been repeatedly lauded as one of the top pilots at Fort Drum.

The Night Stalkers had offered an education in what it really meant to fly. In the two years of her training, she'd flown more hours than in the seven years prior, despite two deployments to Iraq. And she'd spent more time in the classroom than her life-to-date accumulated flight hours.

But she was ready now. It was *très viscérale,*

right down in her bones she could feel it. The Chinook was as much a part of her nervous system as breathing.

Too bad they didn't build men the way they built the big Chinooks—especially the MH-47G which were built specifically to SOAR's requirements. The aircraft were steady, trustworthy, and the most immensely powerful helicopters deployed in the U.S. Army—what more could a girl ask for? But finding a superhero man to go with her superhero helicopter was just a fantasy for a lonely teenage girl.

She dove down into a canyon and slid to a hover mere inches over the reservoir inside the thirty-second window laid out on the flight plan.

Danielle resisted a sigh. She was ready for something to happen and to happen soon.

# # #

Pete's Chinook and his two escort Black Hawks crossed into the mountainous province of Sikkim, India ten feet over the glaciers and still moving fast. It was an hour before dawn, they'd made it out of China while it was still dark.

"Twenty minutes of fuel remaining," Nicolai said it like a personal challenge when they hit the border.

"Thanks, I never would have noticed."

It had been a nail-biting tradeoff: the more fuel he burned, the more easily he climbed due to the lighter load.

The more he climbed, the faster he burned what little fuel remained.

Safe in Indian airspace he climbed hard as Nicolai counted down the minutes remaining, burning fuel even faster than he had been while crossing the mountains of southern Tibet. They caught up with the U.S. Air Force HC-130P Combat King refueling tanker with only ten minutes of fuel left.

"Ram that bitch," Nicolai called out.

Pete extended the refueling probe which reached only a few feet beyond the forward edge of the rotor blade and drove at the basket trailing behind the tanker on its long hose.

He nailed it on the first try despite the fluky winds. Striking the valve in the basket with over four hundred pounds of pressure, a clamp snapped over the refueling probe and Jet A fuel shot into his tanks.

His helo had the least fuel due to having the most men aboard, so he was first in line. His Number Two picked up the second refueling basket trailing off the other wing of the Combat King. Thirty seconds and three hundred gallons later and he was breathing much more easily.

"Ah," Nicolai sighed. "It is better than the sex," his thick Russian accent only ever surfaced in this moment or while picking up women.

"Hey, Nicolai," Nicky the Greek called over the intercom from his crew chief position seated behind Pete. "Do you make love in Russian?"

A question Pete had always been careful to avoid.

"For you, I make special exception." That got a laugh over the system.

Which explained why Pete always kept his mouth shut at this moment.

"The ladies, Nicolai? What about the ladies?" Alfie the portside gunner asked.

"Ah," he sighed happily as he signaled that the other choppers had finished their refueling and formed up to either side, "the ladies love the Russian. They don't need to know I grew up in Maryland and I learn my great-great-grandfather's native tongue at the University called Virginia."

He sounded so pleased that Pete wished he'd done the same rather than study Japanese and Mandarin.

Another two hours of—thank god—straight-and-level flight at altitude through the breaking dawn and they landed on the aircraft carrier awaiting them in the Bay of Bengal. India had agreed to turn a blind eye as long as the Americans never actually touched their soil.

Once standing on the deck—and the worst of the kinks had been worked out—he pulled his team together: six pilots and seven crew chiefs.

"Honor to serve!" He saluted them sharply.

"Hell yeah!" They shouted in response and saluted in turn. It was their version of spiking the football in the end zone.

A petty officer in a bright green vest appeared

at his elbow, "Follow me please, sir." He pointed toward the Navy-gray command structure that towered above the carrier's deck. The Commodore of the entire carrier group was waiting for him just outside the entrance. Not a good idea to keep a One-Star waiting, so he waved at the team.

"See you in the mess for dinner," he shouted to the crew over the noise of an F-18 Hornet fighter jet trapping on the #2 wire. After two days of surviving on MREs while squatting on the Tibetan tundra, he was ready for a steak, a burger, a mountain of pasta...maybe all three.

The green escorted him across the hazards of the busy flight deck. Pete had kept his helmet on to buffer the noise, but even at that he winced as another Hornet fired up and was flung aloft by the catapult.

"Orders, Major Napier," the Commodore handed him a folded sheet the moment he arrived. "Hate to lose you."

The Commodore saluted, which Pete automatically returned before looking down at the sheet of paper in his hands. The man left before the import of Pete's orders slammed in.

A different green-clad deckhand showed up with Pete's duffle bag and began guiding him toward a loading C-2 Greyhound twin-prop airplane. It was parked number two for the launch catapult, close behind the raised jet-blast deflector.

His crew, being led across in the opposite

direction to return to the berthing decks below, looked at him aghast.

"Stateside," was all he managed to gasp out as they passed.

A stream of foul cursing followed him from behind. Their crew was tight. Why the hell was Command breaking it up?

And what in the name of fuck-all had he done to deserve this?

He glanced at the orders again as he stumbled up the Greyhound's rear ramp and crash landed into a seat.

Training rookies?

It was worse than a demotion.

This was punishment.

Target of the Heart *and other titles are available at fine retailers everywhere.*

Other works by M.L. Buchman

<u>**Dead Chef Thrillers**</u>
Swap Out!
One Chef!
Two Chef!

<u>**SF/F Titles**</u>
Nara
Monk's Maze
The Me and Elsie Chronicles

Don't Miss a Thing!
Sign up for M. L. Buchman's newsletter
today
and receive:
Release News
Free Short Stories
a Free Starter Library

Do it today. Do it now.
http://www.mlbuchman.com/newsletter/